A Humpback Whale Tale

adapted by Justin Spelvin

based on the original teleplay by Chris Gifford and Val Walsh

illustrated by Ron Zalme

Simon Spotlight/Nick Jr.
New York   London   Toronto   Sydney

Based on the TV series *Go, Diego, Go!*™ as seen on Nick Jr.®

SIMON SPOTLIGHT
An imprint of Simon & Schuster Children's Publishing Division
1230 Avenue of the Americas, New York, New York 10020
© 2006 Viacom International Inc. All rights reserved. NICK JR., *Go, Diego, Go!*, and all related titles,
logos, and characters are trademarks of Viacom International Inc. All rights reserved, including the right
of reproduction in whole or in part in any form.
SIMON SPOTLIGHT and colophon are registered trademarks of Simon & Schuster, Inc.
Manufactured in the United States of America
First Edition
10 9 8 7 6 5 4 3 2 1
ISBN-13: 978-1-4169-1511-9
ISBN-10: 1-4169-1511-7

First we need to find out who's in trouble. Click the Camera can help. Say "Click!" Click has four pictures of animals. The animal that needs our help says "Aoo ahh, aoo ahh." Do you see an animal like that?

¡Sí! The humpback whale. When humpback whales dive underwater, they bend their backs in a hump shape. But this baby whale is stuck on a rocky island all by himself. We've got to save the baby humpback whale and get him back to his mommy!

¡Al rescate, mis amigos! To the rescue, my friends!

We have to get through these swinging vines without getting tangled in them. Let's bend our backs like humpback whales to go under the vines. Watch out for spiders and snakes!

Great bending! We've got to call to the baby humpback whale to let him know we're coming. Call with me. "Aoo ahh! Aoo ahh!"

Now we need to find the path that leads to the beach. Let's think like scientists. Should we take the path that goes toward the rainforest, toward the mountain, or toward the ocean?

Yeah, this is the path that leads to the beach! We're almost there, but we can't walk on these sand dunes. They are here to protect the beach. We need something to help us fly over them. I know! Rescue Pack can transform into anything I need. Say *"¡Activate!"*

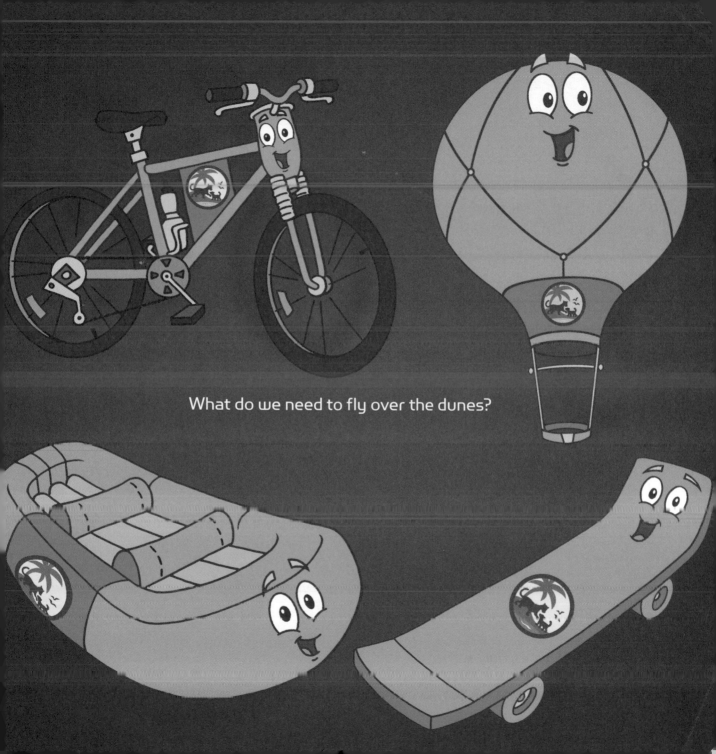

What do we need to fly over the dunes?

A hot-air balloon! *¡Perfecto!*
Oh, no! It's the Bobo Brothers. Those silly monkeys are always causing trouble.
If they keep bouncing on our balloon, we'll never get to the baby humpback whale!

To stop the Bobos we have to clap three times.
Now say "Freeze, Bobos!"

Uh-oh, look! Giant, stinging jellyfish! The jellyfish could sting us, but we've got to get to that whale!

Hey! We can ask my friend Tuga the Leatherback Sea Turtle if we can ride on her back. Jellyfish are scared of leatherback sea turtles.

Tuga speaks Spanish, so to tell Tuga that we need to swim, say *"¡Nademos!"*
Uh-oh! We're being chased by sharks! We'd better swim even faster. *¡Nademos!*
¡Nademos!

We made it! This baby humpback whale needs to get back in the water fast. We can't lift him off the island, but maybe a big wave can.

Humpback whales make really big waves when they splash their tails in the water. Let's call for the humpback whale family to help us make really big waves. Say "Aoo ahh! Aoo ahh!"

Splash, whales, splash!
Look, the big wave is carrying the baby humpback whale back to his mommy!

¡Excellente! We did it! The baby humpback whale is back safe with his family.
¡Mision cumplida! Rescue complete! You're a great Animal Rescuer!

Did you know?

Nice trick!

Humpback whales are the ocean's acrobats. They jump completely out of the water and land on their backs with a terrific splash!

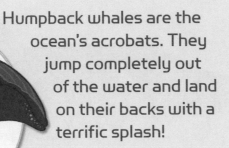

Tiny appetites!

Even though they are so big, humpback whales eat only small fish, and tiny plants and animals.

Long and strong!

Most grown-up humpback whales are about forty feet long. That's about the size of a school bus!

Sweet tunes!

Male humpback whales communicate to female humpback whales by singing.

Tipping the scales!

A fully grown humpback whale weighs about as much as four elephants.